THE ROMAN HEIR

An Argolicus Mystery

ZARA ALTAIR

Fervent
Crux
Press

INTRODUCTION

❧

Thank you for reading *The Roman Heir*.

You wouldn't be here if you didn't like a good mystery and diving into another time.

I'd love to hear from you. Send me a message at zara@zaraaltair.com

Follow me on Twitter @ZaraAltair

If you enjoy *The Roman Heir*, please consider telling your friends and posting a short review. Word of mouth is an author's best friend and much appreciated. Thank you.

Enter the world of Argolicus

With few exceptions, the western world was at peace in the year 512 after Christ's birth. Warlords were plotting in the Balkans either for the East or the West, but mainly for their own power. Rumblings in Persian borderlands perhaps threatened the Roman Empire as seated in Constantinople. The most recent disturbances—betrayals, if you will—of the

Frankish kingdoms had been settled some five years. Bishops and clergy squabbled over textual interpretations of the Gospel, patristic writings, or Patriarchal proclamations, as usual, some in a huff, others with conciliatory leanings. Vandals had controlled northern Africa for almost 100 years. The Visigoths ruled Spain and traded with avarice. In Italy affairs of concern were mainly internal—the parallel Roman law and Ostrogoth legal systems ran under the regal Edicts guided by a sense of civility, providing structure for dispute resolution.

CHAPTER 1
LEAVING ROME

The words were not as cold as the Roman winter air, but they stung Argolicus.

"You see," Boethius said, leaning toward Argolicus in a confidential manner, "Rome is a closed community. When someone like you whose family lineage is not from one of the great families of Rome and as a newcomer attempts to take on a centuries-old Roman position, you set yourself up for strife. You are wise to retire, go back to your provincial Bruttia and live as local nobility."

Argolicus watched from the palatial villa on the Caelian Hill as gentle snowflakes fell on the city and the forum below. He stood on a balcony where Boethius had led him just minutes before. Behind them loomed a grand study filled with manuscripts and books. Boethius carefully peeled an apple, the skin curling off onto the floor at his feet. Argolicus knew everything Boethius was saying and they echoed his reasons for leaving. He also knew Boethius, so he waited for him to get to the point.

"The same talents that make you a good judge," Boethius continued, "hamper your political power. You read people, you consider all possibilities, you listen carefully to all sides, you weigh outcomes. In politics you must make a decision, move quickly, ignore repercussions, and strike."

Argolicus recognized his political failings and felt the sting of being blocked on more than one occasion by the powerful families of Rome and the prelates of the Church.

"Go back to your home, enjoy your studies," Boethius said as he cut off a small section of apple. "I have a parting gift for you." He bent to the table and lifted a book, handing it to Argolicus. One of the richest men in Rome, Boethius loved books as much as Argolicus did, perhaps even more.

Argolicus looked down at the small book, almost a pamphlet, but covered in leather.

"I translated it," Boethius said, as he looked down at the book. "Aristotle's *Categories*. I know you are one of the few left who read Greek, but I thought you might like it for your collection."

Truly pleased, Argolicus smiled. "Thank you. I will read it in solitude without the endless sessions of reading Greek aloud."

"Ah, Nikolaos," Boethius said, reading Argolicus' mind, "he is a taskmaster." Argolicus' tutor and lifelong companion waited for Argolicus somewhere in the villa.

"He is," Argolicus said smiling, "but without him my Greek would suffer." The two men stood looking out over a wintry Rome.

"I'm wondering," Boethius said, "Are you going by ship? Or by land?"

"Oh, quickly, by sea. Portus to Squillace."

"Then I'd ask you for a favor."

"Yes?"

"I have another copy for a young scholar. I'm wondering if you could deliver it for me. Books are so precious, I dislike just sending them. Plus, you would like the lad. He loves to read and think."

"Why? Where is he?"

"He lives in Ostia in the old family villa, a large *domus* in the center of the city. His father is a friend of Symmachus and I thought..."

Ah, here it was, politics. Even as he was leaving Rome one last push.

"Of course, I'll take it. We were leaving in four days, but I could leave tomorrow and stop to deliver the book. What's his name?"

"Servius Norbanus Philo. He is the son of Pius."

Argolicus knew this errand tied him to Roman aristocracy, another wealthy and old family. Servius Norbanus Pius had inherited a shipping business that had grown with the stability of King Theodoric's rule. In Rome, his home was near Boethius' on the Caelian Hill, but one of the reasons for his success was his constant presence in Ostia near the huge shipping center Portus to personally oversee the shipping business. "Philo," he said. "I shall make sure he receives your gift."

SERVIUS NORBANUS PHILO MET ARGOLICUS IN HIS FATHER'S study and office. The young man was lost amid a collection of carved ivory, large enameled plaques, colored glass vases, marble figurines, brass figurines, gold figurines, cast bronze sculptures, tiny enamel boxes, gilt boxes set with gems, silver trinkets, and one elephant tusk displayed on a high shelf. He appeared very young, seventeen or so. His dark brown eyes were fringed with long, equally dark lashes. His dark hair was cut in the Roman style like a cap around his head and his olive complexion was sallow with grief and shock. He looked at the book Argolicus had handed to him with a blank stare.

"My father was killed this morning. I can't focus. Boethius is kind," he said in a deep, rich voice belying his slight stature. "I shall write my thanks." He looked up from the book. His gaze slid over Nikolaos, Argolicus' tutor slave, who stood waiting near the entry from the *atrium* next to a large marble statue of Venus. Finally, he focused on Argolicus. "And you are kind to take time to make a delivery in your period of transition."

"Boethius has a way of getting his way," Argolicus said, smiling. "But it was no inconvenience."

"He does," Philo said. "I wish I had half of his persuasive talent, because, right now, I'd like to ask your help." He looked as though tears were near.

"My help?"

"Yes. Even I know your reputation. You discover things, you know people, you treat all parties fairly..."

"Philo, I'm flattered by your admiration, but I have left my appointment in Rome. I'm here in Ostia to go home without any title. I have the family estate. I am uncomfortable as it is, intruding on your family when your father was found murdered just this morning. I feel I have no place here."

"There, you see," Philo said. "What if Boethius were asking you for the same request? How would he ask you? My father's been killed and I need your help. Blood. There was so much blood." He closed his eyes.

Argolicus thought the boy was not as inept at manipulation as he believed he was. "Why not use the local Promagistrate. Who knows what this investigation will take?"

"He's on vacation in the south chasing the warm weather. Our family's left with the local militia. They narrow their activities to apprehension, not investigation."

Argolicus felt the draw of a puzzle, pulled in a breath, and glanced at Nikolaos. "Where did it happen?"

"Right behind your slave, in the *atrium*. I was coming to meet him before he got busy. He said I was too young to go to the Games in Rome by myself. I wanted to ask him one more time. It's January, young people have fun. I wanted to know what it's like to be free for just a few days."

Nikolaos was already in the *atrium* examining the dizzying mosaic pattern on the floor. His middle-aged but lithe body moved as he scanned the expansive floor.

Philo said, "We moved the body and cleaned the floor. He probably won't find anything."

"Where is your father's body now? May I look at it? We can leave my tutor to discover what he will in the *atrium*," Argolicus asked, submitting to the pull of the murder and solving the puzzle. As much as Servius Norbanus Pius was a private citizen, his shipping business kept Rome supplied with goods. Murder was a private family matter under the law, but when it affected the public good then the Promagistrate initiated public legal investigations.

The young man came out from behind the large table covered in papers and trinkets, and appeared to grow in stature and age, separated from his father's large collection. His golden-toned voice resonated among the treasures. "He's in a *cubiculum*."

Philo strode out of the large study, across the *atrium*, and led Argolicus to a small room on the opposite side. Servius Norbanus Pius was laid out on a table, his body was stripped, and slaves were washing with care.

"Ask them to leave," Argolicus said. He crossed the room to the body.

"I... I can't look," Philo said, and rushed from the room.

The body was deep pink on top—face, chest, thighs—and white on the bottom along the back. Blood had settled as Pius lay face down on the ground. Argolicus saw five stab wounds in his chest and a large slash across the man's neck. Why didn't Philo mention how brutal this was? Bruises marked his shoulders and arms, spotting purple against the white skin. Argolicus picked up the right hand. The fingers and wrist were stiff, but he saw scrapes and raw patches around the knuckles, and the right palm was slashed. He moved around the table. The left hand was also marked with scrapes but was clutched tight and closed. Argolicus tried opening the fingers to see what was in the grip, but the fingers were too stiff to move. He stood back for an overview and a sadness at the human condition overwhelmed him as he looked at the evidence of violence.

When he left the room, he found Philo sitting on the edge of the pool in the *atrium*. Tiny snowflakes glittered in the light as they fell into the pool. The pale winter light from the open roof overhead highlighted the youth's body hunkered in dejection. Philo looked up as Argolicus crossed to the pool. "I couldn't bear to see him... like that. And the punctures in his skin. The body looked like my father, but it wasn't my father. It was a thing." He stood up to face Argolicus. His face was set and grim, seeming to have lost the sorrow when he first met Argolicus.

"The death was violent," Argolicus said, still in his sorrow for the human condition. "It is hard to see. I've seen more than one. Each time I feel sorrow, guilt, shame for our condition. The first dead body I saw was my father. Although he was not murdered, I remember how I felt. I was about your age."

Philo's eyes widened and he blurted, "He was? The first dead body? Your father?"

"He was. I know how you feel. I will help you until it is time for me to meet the boat. Maybe, by then, the magistrate will arrive."

Philo looked relieved. "My sister is with my mother. My uncle will be here soon from Portus."

Argolicus said, "I will speak with everyone."

"Yes. My uncle has his own family, but my father was pater familias." He nodded toward a statue near the back wall of the *atrium*, a likeness of Pius fully clothed and looking regal. A slave quietly crossed the *atrium* toward the back bedrooms glancing at Philo.

"I'll talk to them all later. From the state of his body it looks as though your father died in the early morning. Did you hear anything?"

"No. My room is upstairs." Philo nodded toward the back wall of the *atrium*. "Father's room is downstairs. There would have to be a lot of noise for me to hear something."

"Master," Nikolaos called from the garden. "Master, I have found something."

Philo and Argolicus hurried to the *peristylum*. Argolicus saw the main courtyard, the large pool, columns surrounding the pool, and a garden with many bare shrubs and some small plants surrounding the marble courtyard.

"Over here," called Nikolaos. He stood up in the corner of the room near the other passageway from the *atrium*. "There's blood here on the ground, and splatters on the marble."

Philo blurted, "But I found him in the *atrium*."

"We'll look," Argolicus said as he moved toward Nikolaos. Philo followed with a puzzled frown.

"Here," Nikolaos said and pointed to the ground.

Argolicus looked down and saw the blood, now mostly dry splattered on the leaves of a small plant, on the soil in the ground, and splatters on the marble. He looked to the left and saw the hallway to the servant entrance. "Is that locked at night?"

Philo nodded his head. "Yes, the porter locks it and then goes to his room by the vestibule and the front door."

Argolicus looked at the blood and saw light smears here and there in the *atrium* passageway where someone had tried to wipe up the blood. "Where did you find your father?"

Philo looked through the passageway to the *atrium* and pointed. "Straight ahead, by the *atrium* pool."

As Argolicus followed his direction, a young woman entered the passageway. The first image that came to his mind was a lioness. Her hair was lighter than Philo's, backlit by the light from the *atrium* ceiling it shone in gold highlights. Her skin was honeyed. Her lips and cheeks glowed rose like a plump peach. Her blue tunic, laced with gold cords, revealed inviting curves.

"Philo, are you entertaining a guest, now? Mother wants you."

"Titiana, this is Gaius Vitellius Argolicus. He's come from Rome to bring a gift from Boethius."

Titiana smiled. "Let me guess. A book."

CHAPTER 2

FAMILY MATTERS

Aemilia Atia sat straight in her chair. She looked directly at Argolicus. "My husband had a certain verve for life," Aemilia Atia said. She was a striking woman approaching fifty, with handsome features echoed by Titiana, sitting next to her. Argolicus could tell she was used to being in charge. "His brother, Sabinus, is more down to earth."

Aemilia Atia, Philo's mother, had left her bedroom and gathered everyone in the entertainment room when she learned of the guest. The floor was covered in a dizzying array of black and white mosaics and the walls were painted with intricate scenes of trees and flowers and young people playing musical instruments in nature. Braziers, next to seats, warmed the room from the winter cold. Slaves brought trays of *gustum*: small tidbits of fruit, cheese, and salads for nibbling placed on platters and bowls around the seats, but no one was eating.

"He was a collector. You saw his study. There are storage rooms filled with more. He rotated items so he could enjoy it all bit by bit." She gazed at the wall behind Argolicus. "He had the walls repainted to make them more lively." She looked down at Titiana's clasped hands and placed her be-ringed fingers over her daughter's. Titiana leaned closer.

Argolicus was about to ask her a question, when she continued. "He collected people as well. He worked at developing connections... of all kinds."

Argolicus asked, "Can you think of anyone who would want to injure him?"

Aemilia Atia gazed into a middle distance. "He wasn't always loved. He was ruthless in bargains. But, no. I can't think of anyone who would want to do this." She waved in the direction of the *cubiculum*.

Titiana shifted, her eyes opening wide. "He was..." She stopped, looking at Philo who said nothing. He sat with the glazed look he'd had when Argolicus arrived.

Argolicus waited, but none of them spoke.

Aemilia suddenly broke from her reverie, "Please, eat. You must be hungry after your trip from Rome. This is no time to lose courtesy. Perhaps it is even more important now." She picked a grape and nibbled off a tiny piece.

Once she had picked up the grape, Philo was the first to reach for a small pastry. Argolicus looked at the array of delicacies on the tray next to his seat: eggs in pine nut sauce, a small dish of asparagus cooked in eggs and herbs, a pastry. He picked up the pastry and took a bite: roasted lamb bits with herbs and pine nuts. As soon as he took a bite, a slave appeared with a light translucent blue glass goblet filled with honeyed wine and placed it on the table next to the tray.

"Father was a busy man," Philo said. "Every morning he received people here in his study to conduct business. But in the afternoons and evenings he was often gone. He was very social."

Titiana sighed and pulled away from her mother's shoulder.

Aemilia drew up her shoulders. "He wasn't a family man."

Argolicus waited for more.

Aemilia continued, "He was always out visiting. Sometimes he came home with a new acquisition. He kept the newest ones on his desk so he could admire them. When he arranged dinner parties here the guests often included new people we had not met before. As exotic as his collection items are... were, he never invited anyone who was not a Roman."

Philo added, "Yes, they had long conversations into the night about Theodoric and his People. He made certain his guests were from old families. They talked about the new appointees from the King. He called them upstarts. They would scheme and plan. But, it was all talk. That's how he and Boethius became friends."

Argolicus once again was glad he was leaving the enclave of Romans. "How do you feel about the King?" he asked.

"Me?" Philo said. "I prefer my books to politics. I have no experience of the 'old ways,' as my father reverently called them. Maybe I'm young. Going to the Games on my own was an adventure for me." He paused. "But I see that it won't happen this year."

Aemilia said, "There will be other years, Philo. Now you are the man of the house. We must make funeral arrangements. You need to learn from Sabinus. You'll be busy now. I'm sure the new Consul, Flavius Paulus, won't miss you at the Games."

"Sabinus?" Argolicus said. The talk was wandering from Pius' death. He felt the time constraint before his boat left. If he could get a better picture of the family he was certain he would find clues to Pius' violent death.

Aemilia drew up her shoulders and then let them down. "Sabinus is a businessman. An organizer. His life is the port. His daily activities are filled with cargo and the coming and going of ships. He makes certain cargo is distributed to make room for what is contained in the new ships that arrive. He rarely attends social events and even more rarely hosts them. He spends the evenings with his family." She paused. Argolicus saw a tiny frown develop between her elegant eyebrows.

"He is devoted to his family. He has three boys and two girls. He has a penchant for the ordinary and the pedestrian. I've heard him tell the story of Cornelia's jewels in reference to his own children. What can I say? His home is in Portus; his work is in Portus. Pius thought him boring. But, he did make the shipping business run smoothly."

Argolicus waited to see if Titiana or Philo had anything to add, but they were both silent each seemingly lost in their own thoughts.

"And you?" Argolicus asked, looking directly at Aemilia. "How did you get along with Pius?"

"What do you mean 'get along'?" Aemilia asked. "We were husband and wife. We made things work."

Argolicus waited without responding.

Aemilia shrugged. "We were amicable. I wouldn't say we were a loving couple. We've been married many years. We made it work."

Philo stared blankly. Titiana moved away from her mother and sat primly alone.

"Did you argue?" Argolicus asked.

"Of course, we argued. We were a couple. We had our disagreements but I can't recall any arguments of any seriousness. Marital disagreements happen with any couple." Before Argolicus could speak she said, "I don't know who you are trying to ensnare. Philo asked you to look into his death, but I won't suffer insinuations from anyone, especially just the kind of man my husband could not tolerate."

She drew up her shoulders again, stood up, and began to leave the room.

Argolicus stood as well, mentally brushing off her reference to his appointment in Rome. To her he was one of the new Romans whose appointment came from the King. "I am sorry I have upset you. Murder is upsetting. I ask questions. The more I know the better I understand."

Aemilia said, "I'll leave you to Philo."

Titiana stood, glanced at Philo, and then ran across the room. Both of her fists beat Argolicus on the chest. "You don't understand anything," she cried as she hit him over and over.

Philo jumped up from his silent reverie to pull Titiana away. She turned and sobbed into her brother's shoulder. Then she ran out of the room.

Philo looked at Argolicus. His face was distorted like a young child about to cry. "I apologize for my mother and my sister. My father protected them from the world. They feel exposed and defenseless."

"I'm sure they do," Argolicus said. "And you?"

Philo seemed to gather himself. "We are a family. We are not a loving family. My father kept the household running. We all bowed to his will. Even Sabinus. He was pater familias, but at a distance. What my mother said was right, they were married like the contractual arrangement that they made from the beginning. She did his bidding and relied on him for protection."

He stopped. Then he waved his arm at the house before them. "Look at this. Look at all of it. This is a house of things. To my father, people were a means to an end and the end was things. I was his son and I was his possession. I must always look good. I'm sure the reason he didn't want me to go to Rome was not because of anything that would happen, but because young people do wild things and he did not want me to do anything that would reflect on his name."

"And your books?" Argolicus asked. "Did he approve of your library?"

"Yes and no. He approved of the collection. My building my own collection was an extension of his image. But my 'bookishness,' as he called it, upset him. He wanted me to be more of a man."

"A man? What does that mean?" Argolicus asked.

"To be like him, of course. To take the family name out in public. To attend events. To go to parties. To accompany him on his searches for the one new thing. That's what he meant. He cited Boethius as an example of a man who loved books and yet was in the thick of things."

Argolicus had a picture now of the young man's emotional turmoil. His father was dead and he had no one to help. He'd been pushed into a position he couldn't handle and that did not suit his nature. "Ah, to be a man in his image."

"Yes, exactly. My father wanted me to be just like him. I'm not."

"Philo, do you want me to stay and continue? I don't want to upset your mother or your sister."

"Yes, more than ever. You saw how emotional they are. How would they help find who killed my father?" He nodded toward the passageway where Aemilia and Titiana had disappeared. "I need you." He looked Argolicus in the eye.

Argolicus felt an ache at the bottom of his chest at the remembrance of his own father's death. He also remembered the comfort he had taken in the male presence of his uncle, not only a book lover, but a maker of books. He nodded.

"Oh, I am grateful," Philo exclaimed like a young child. "I can't make a fancy speech, but I thank you from the bottom of my lheart."

Argolicus felt that pain in his chest dissipate. "I will do as much as I can do."

"In that case, I know the perfect room for you here in the house. Let me show you." He led Argolicus out of the entertainment room into the *peristylum* and turned left toward a set of stairs at the far end. "I know it is old-fashioned, but I have a tutor, too. He's probably in my library looking for something for us to read this evening. His name is Bion."

Nikolaos appeared from somewhere in the *peristylum* and followed them up the stairs. At the top of the stairs was a long hallway lined with doorways.

"I like it up here," Philo said. "The rooms have windows. They are light during the day." He led them along the corridor to a door and opened it. Inside the door was a small whitewashed room for Nikolaos and beyond that a brightly painted *cubiculum* set with a bed, a chair, and two small tables. One held a wash basin and small linens; the other was slightly larger to serve as a desk with two oil lamps. A brazier stood near the table against the winter chill. The walls were painted here and there with figures: young women and men singing and cavorting among trees and one lone shepherd playing his pipe.

Argolicus found his travel bag already placed in a corner. "Thank you, Philo. This will do nicely."

"Oh, there is more I want to show you. My library is next door." He nodded his head to toward the left. "Once you are settled, I'll show you my collection." His face shown with pride.

"Perhaps after dinner. We can all read together."

"I like that idea," Philo said. "We can read from the new book." He looked around the room and hesitated.

Argolicus said, "We'll be fine. I'll arrange my things. Then I'll take a walk and do some thinking. Where will you be in a couple of hours?"

"I'm sure I'll be in my father's study. Uncle Sabinus is due in the next hour. We'll have many things to discuss."

"I'll join you there. I want to speak with your uncle." He watched the young man leave. Was I ever that vulnerable?

He must have said it aloud because Nikolaos said, "Yes, Master."

CHAPTER 3
NOTHING REVEALED

A rgolicus sighed. "I thought I was leaving all this."
Nikolaos looked toward the end of the street.
"Just two more days after this."
They were walking toward the edge of Ostia and the ocean. The streets were lined with empty shops and vacant apartment buildings. For the past 200 years, Ostia had ceased to be a thriving port, the harbor silted in, and what remained was country retreats for rich Romans. Buildings in disuse showed signs of crumbling from neglect. The snow had melted but a wind from the ocean blew cold, carrying the scent of the sea. Argolicus pulled his cloak tighter.

"I think I would not have liked Pius. Demanding and supercilious. It seems his collection was all he cared about. He didn't seem to care for his family except as an obligation. And the mother, Aemilia, is so cold. I'm sure Pius was a difficult man. But, she paints a picture of a model Roman family. The daughter is right. I don't understand. The boy is the best of the lot."

They reached the end of the street. What used to be the harbor was a silted marsh. Reeds bent in waves as the wind rushed in from the water. They turned and walked along the edge of the marsh.

Nikolaos said, "The daughter, Titiana, seemed overwrought. Hitting you is not a typical Roman action. She's not a child. She looks close to twenty. Old enough to know that what she did is not acceptable."

Argolicus breathed on his cold fingers. "I can't tell if she is upset at the loss of her father or terrified of the murder. Her words 'you don't understand' could mean anything. Did she love her father? Was Pius more strict with her than with Philo? It all seems as muddy as this marsh."

He watched the reeds blowing lost in his thoughts of the family. He heard Nikolaos turn.

Nikolaos cried, "Hup."

Argolicus turned and began to raise his arms from his cape but the blow landed just above his solar plexus. Air whooshed out and he couldn't breathe. He found he was sitting on the ground. His diminutive tutor stood over him shaking his graying hair.

"Master, you must learn to quicken your response. Even though Romans cannot carry arms under King Theodoric, knowing defense is important."

Argolicus looked up from his sitting position on the ground, took in a couple of breaths, and said, "I don't know which is worse; your endless Greek conjugations or your fight training. Right now I think it's the training." He took in a few more breaths, then got up. "Time to go back and meet this Sabinus."

❧

SABINUS AND PHILO WERE IN THE STUDY. PHILO LOOKED UP when Argolicus entered. Nikolaos took his position alongside Venus.

"Argolicus, I was just telling my uncle how Titiana struck you. Uncle, this is Gaius Vitellius Argolicus, ex praefect of Rome."

"Numerius Norbanus Sabinus, Your Sublimity." Sabinus gave a brief nod tending toward a bow. A short man, in his mid forties with a gleaming bald dome surrounded by dark curls, Sabinus had the air of a man of business. His tunic was plain but made of finely woven wool. Argolicus saw no jewelry. The man's direct gaze emphasized his erect posture. A man of facts and transactions from head to toe.

Philo continued, "My sister has been distraught lately. I don't know why. For the past couple of weeks she's been on edge, bursting into tears or blinking back anger for no reason. Father's death has exacerbated her reactions."

Argolicus said, "Everyone reacts differently to death. And murder compounds the feelings. Your sister is young." He decided to lead the conversation somewhere else. He glanced at the desk. "Are you planning the funeral?"

Sabinus answered, "Yes, it will be small. The priest here will conduct the liturgy. I've arranged for the burial in Rome."

"Sabinus," Argolicus said. "Would you be willing to look at your brother's body with me? To tell me if you notice anything. You saw him regularly."

Sabinus looked uneasy, but said, "Yes, I can look. But what do you think I will see? Pius is dead."

"That's just the point. If you could tell me anything you might notice that is different."

Sabinus nodded. They headed across the *atrium* to look at Pius.

In the *cubiculum*, Sabinus gasped. "He's so pink."

"Yes," Argolicus said. "A disturbing manifestation of death."

Sabinus walked to the edge of the table. "Who would do this? Five stab wounds." He touched each one. "And his neck. Did someone try to cut his throat? This is hard to see."

"Are you all right? It was a vicious killing. "

"Yes, yes," Sabinus answered. "It's upsetting. It looks like Pius and it doesn't. My brother." He bent over Pius' body and sobbed.

Argolicus watched in silence, sensing the man's grief.

Sabinus straightened, touched Pius' face, and turned to Argolicus. "No, I don't see anything that looks different to me."

They turned toward the door and entered the *atrium*.

THE DOORMAN, N'GOLO, WAS DARK, POWERFUL, AND compact as a draft horse, and imposing as though the heavy air of the jungle was wrapped around his being.

"I'm here all night," he said, gesturing to his room off the entry. "No one could get past me. The sound of them pounding on the door would wake the entire household. Look at that thick beam. The doors are heavy. Someone knocks, I open the door. That's how people get in."

"I am not questioning your trustworthiness," Argolicus said. "I'm wondering how someone, not part of this household, could get access to Pius."

N'Golo relaxed his glare. "Why don't you ask the cook, Vasilios? Now there's someone who enjoys being in charge. He lords it over the cooks. He seeks a perfect world unattainable by the rest of us. Ask him, because he and his slaves go in and out the *posticum* at all hours of the day and night bringing goods in and taking out waste. If you are looking for someone who could have left a door open giving access into the house, look no further than the kitchen." He crossed his arms over his massive chest.

Argolicus was soon in the kitchen where the overwhelming heat of the cooking fires contrasted with the cool winter air in the *atrium*. Dinner preparations were well under way. Vasilios, although not tall, was recognizable from his constant stream of commands as he paced around the work tables. "Don't stop stirring. Small bits, small bits, we're not feeding lions. Stop! Don't put that on until the coals are just right." He noticed the invader, Argolicus, enter the door. "Yes?"

"Vasilios? Could we speak for a few minutes?" Argolicus asked.

"I can't leave. Not even for a moment." He glanced toward a table. "Not yet! Wait until the egg has thickened the sauce completely."

Argolicus walked into the kitchen.

"On second thought," Vasilios said, visibly upset. "Let's talk in the corner there by the pantry."

Argolicus joined him at the arched entry to the pantry where shelves full of urns and herbs towered toward the ceiling. "I'm wondering if any of your staff went out the *posticum* in the early morning."

"Of course," Vasilios answered. "Magda goes out to the fish market when the boats come in. Little Rufus takes the waste to the barges. Gently, gently, Magda. The white fish is delicate. Ali is at the meat market before the butchers. I get the best of everything there is in Ostia."

"Early this morning, who, specifically, went out?"

Vasilios cast his eyes over Argolicus' shoulder. "No, no, no. The pastry must sit quietly before it is filled. This morning? Well, Magda for certain. She's preparing the fish now." He grimaced and called. "Demetrius and the martyrs! Rufus, the grapes go on top, not first." He shook his head in a dramatic suffering effect. "You see? I can't leave them for a moment."

Argolicus wondered who had suffered most for the light meal he'd eaten earlier with the family. "Anyone else?"

Vasilios pondered for a moment, his eyes never leaving his industrious workers. "Junia," he called. A young woman left off chopping beets into tiny cubes. "Did you go out with Magda this morning? Ali, prepare another dove, that glutton Sabinus is here."

Junia nodded her head and went back to chopping.

"Just you and Magda?"

Junia nodded again.

Argolicus said, "I'll speak with Magda for a moment. Thank you, Vasilios."

Vasilios nodded as he returned to the work tables. "Peak under the cloth, Rufus. Those pastries must be ready now. Magda, talk to His Sublimity."

Magda did not remember anything unusual from the morning.

Thinking that talking to people in a group situation was not proving fruitful, Argolicus arranged to interview the rest of the staff, one by one in his room. He spoke with Bion, Philo's tutor, and also with Pius' ancient tutor but neither shed any light on the early morning hours. He spoke with household slaves and personal attendants of Aemilia and Titiana. He discovered that the boy, Rufus, had the thankless task of collecting night soil from the rooms, but that happened after the household was up and about. In short, the day's result was dead ends.

He sat in his room looking at his notes. "Someone knows something."

"Master," Nikolaos responded, "I agree, but I'm as confounded as you are."

"Well, I am saddened to tell Philo we've uncovered nothing. The person who was closest to Pius, his old tutor Ioses, wouldn't hear an earthquake. His hearing is so bad, he wouldn't have heard Pius leave the room."

Nikolaos chuckled, "Ah, when you are older, you'll have more freedom."

Argolicus raised an eyebrow and smiled. Then his face became serious. "I don't see anyone in this household being angry enough to produce the violence. Five stab wounds. That shows fury, not cold calculation. Sabinus was in Portus. The mother disliked him, tolerated him, but wouldn't want to lose the power. Titiana is hard to read, but I don't see her angry enough. Philo respected him and doesn't seem angry enough, either. A slave or assassin could have been bribed or paid, but then the killing would have been different, not multiple angry stabs, something else."

Nikolaos said, "But it must have been someone he knew. Why else would he meet someone in the middle of the night? And what Roman would be carrying arms, like a dagger, at risk of breaking the law?"

Argolicus looked at his notes from the interviews with the household. There was something, but he couldn't put his finger on it. "It's puzzling. Perhaps it had something to do with his business. We'll go back with Sabinus tomorrow and meet the merchants at Portus."

Nikolaos nodded.

Argolicus rose. "It's time to join the family."

BION READ, "THESE ARE THE PROPERTIES OF THE RATIONAL soul; it sees itself..."

Argolicus, Philo, and Sabinus gathered in Philo's library after a somber dinner. Aemilia had been tight-lipped, Titiana sullen, and Philo submerged in sorrow. Sabinus attempted conversation to no avail. As Bion read Marcus Aurelius, the rationality of the text seemed to sooth everyone in the room.

Old Ioses nodded his head in approval of the choice and leaned toward Bion to hear the words.

Sabinus rose, interrupting the quiet flow of words and thoughts. "It's been a tumultuous day. I'm retiring. Philo, sleep well. We'll take care of everything in due course. Argolicus, tomorrow we're off to Portus."

"We are. Thank you," Argolicus said as Sabinus left him with Philo and the tutors. He agreed. What had begun as a mere gift delivery had transformed into a death investigation with no clues in sight.

Philo said, "Marcus Aurelius was so even and reasonable. I'm in turmoil. My father is dead. I'm suddenly the pater familias and I don't know what to do next."

Argolicus nodded as Bion closed the book and set it aside on a shelf. "Learn from Sabinus. Trust we'll discover what happened."

"Yes, but the politics and the shipping business. My biggest concern was going to the Consular Games and now that sounds so trivial. I need to go among the affairs of men and I feel unready."

Argolicus replied. "I felt the same way when my father died. You will work your way through the complications. Weeks before he died, my father told me there are two kinds of politicians: the ones who seek the truth and the ones who hide it. I've found if I look to determine what type of man I'm dealing with, I know how to move.

Philo frowned and said, "My father said: secrets flow out of the posticum the way goods come in."

CHAPTER 4
PORTUS

Gray overhead cleared to bright winter sunlight as Sabinus directed his boat toward the harbor of Portus. They entered from a small canal from the Tiber river rather than from the ocean like the big transport ships. The great octagon of protected water, designed by Claudius and completed by Trajan, sparkled as the water rippled under the sun. However much, Ostia was a neglected port, the town of Portus and the harbor thrived. Argolicus lifted his palm to shade his eyes.

Ships loading and unloading cargo lined the eight straight sides of the harbor, designed to service the maximum number of ships. Behind the quay, rectangular lines of huge warehouses lined the harbor on every side and beyond. Stevedores scrambled and hauled boxes of fabric and clothing, great amphorae of oil, sacks of grain, and more amphorae filled with wine from ships into the warehouses.

Sabinus pointed to a system of imposing warehouses to their right filling up space beside one side of the octagonal harbor. "Those are our warehouses."

Nikolaos, who sat at the rear of the boat, gasped.

Two large ships were tied up along the quay, masts and spars bare, as stevedores called, grunted, and moved the wares. A tall wooden crane with a pulley attached to a wheel taller than a man, was lifting a large amphora from the docked ship as a worker struggled against the wheel.

Argolicus watched as their boat neared the quay. The closer they came, the larger the warehouses seemed. Everything here illustrated the family held power and control in shipping goods. Philo was not only pater familias but a rich and powerful young man. Does he realize his political sway? Or, the immense wealth he controls? From his bearing, Argolicus felt the youth did not understand his new position in the world, from son to magnate.

"How often did Pius come here?" Argolicus asked.

"Not often," Sabinus said. "He has a personal storage space here. He came for that. Oh, several times a month. I manage the day-to-day operations. There, do you see that big Syrian?" He pointed to the quay. A large man in oriental dress was pacing back and forth shouting orders toward one ship, then checking goods as they went toward the warehouse.

"Yes."

"That's Rashad. He says he is Christian, just like you do. But he sees Christ as a man who united with divinity."

Argolicus held his breath, hoping that they would avoid a contentious discussion on the nature of Christ. Sabinus was a Trinitarian, Argolicus by faith followed the Arian two natures of Christ, and now a Syrian Monophysite. He said, "The Emperor Zeno..."

But before he could finish, Sabinus interrupted him. "My mistake. I didn't mean ill. It's just that we know you are of Their Faith. Whatever King Theodoric proclaims, we try to keep remarks on the natures of Christ out of conversations here at the wharf. Our workers come from all over the world."

Argolicus relaxed. Rashad had noticed the boat coming from the canal. He waved and sent two workers over to help tie up the boat. Their boat sat low under the quay. Big transport ships dwarfed the small vessel as stevedores let down a rope ladder. Nikolaos was last to climb the ladder, looking unsettled.

Argolicus patted the little man's shoulder. "I see you are getting ready for our journey home." The joke passed by the tutor who seemed relieved to have the solid stone pavement of the quay under his feet.

"Rashad, my guest for the day, Gaius Vitellius Argolicus." For a brief instant the big man's green eyes met Argolicus' gaze. Argolicus saw intelligence and hard-edged determination. Then, Rashad dropped his head in a slight bow.

Sabinus continued, "Has The Siren arrived?"

Rashad pointed to a ship anchored in the harbor.

"Good, good," Sabinus said, nodding approval. "Finish with these two so we can bring her in." Rashad nodded and left to direct the stevedores.

"A good man," Sabinus continued. "He speaks the waterfront vernacular which seems to comprise words from many languages. I haven't mastered it. I don't know what I would do without him. Well, let me show you the warehouses."

Sabinus led them toward the arched entrance to the largest warehouse. They passed through the entryway with the family name on a marble slab above into a large courtyard. "This is our family warehouse."

He led them to a locked vestibule. A slave saw Sabinus approach and began to unlock the door. He unlocked a padlock attached to a bolt at the bottom of a large diagonal timber that crossed the door. He pulled out the bolt allowing the beam to move. Then he pushed the slanted beam across a fitted groove in the floor until it stood at a vertical on the left side of the doorway. The enormous responsibility of warehouse owners to secure the goods stored surprised and impressed Argolicus.

"Security is our signature." Sabinus continued as they crossed a vestibule and the slave unlocked a second door. "Pius made sure that everyone knew we take the greatest care to protect merchandise when it arrives," Sabinus said. "A warehouse without security is asking to be robbed."

They entered a large courtyard filled with a black and white mosaic featuring a lion and sheaves of wheat. Sabinus led them across the courtyard to a doorway. "This is the office," he said, gesturing them inside. Two long tables filled the enormous room where clerks sat shuffling papers and ticking off shipping arrivals, storage, and transportation from the warehouse.

"How much of this does Philo understand?" Argolicus asked. The immensity of the enterprise—the ships arriving and departing, the storage, the transportation to destinations throughout Italy—stunned him and would be massive detail to Philo.

"He is learning, but his father wanted him in society so he has only the barest essentials of how it works."

"So, what will happen now?"

"I can suggest, but Philo must make his own decision on how much he wants to be involved. To him it seems as though everything came through his father. Because his personality is not... suited... to mingling and politics, I think he would do well here. But he is a novice. My sons know more than he does. Pius pushed the boy to model his life in his father's image. When I talked to him yesterday, I realized how little he understands."

A young man entered the office. Sabinus smiled. "Larcius, meet Gaius Vitellius Argolicus. He's the one looking into Pius' death. Argolicus, my son."

Larcius looked like Sabinus but with more hair and fewer pounds. As he smiled, Argolicus realized he had the same open nature as his father. "My uncle," he said and then paused. "Philo will be a different man now." He stopped again and glanced at his father as if he had said too much. "Pater, you know how Pius controlled him. He never had a chance to be a boy."

Sabinus said nothing, but his face showed he agreed. "Larcius, the Siren is in the harbor. Get the bills of lading ready. I'll show our guest around."

Larcius mumbled something, picked up a sheet of numbers, and headed to a large desk table at the far end of the office. Larcius, raised at the port, tackled the charts and tables of numbers spread out around the room.

Argolicus said, "I'd like to see Pius' storeroom."

"Storerooms," Sabinus corrected. "He has three. Follow me."

As they crossed the courtyard again, a slave came at a signal from Sabinus. They walked toward the far end of the warehouse. Sabinus nodded toward a door and the slave ran ahead to unfasten the bolt that held the locking beam in place.

The richness at the *domus* in Ostia was paltry compared to the treasures in the storage room. Boxes piled high against the wall of one side almost obscured the light from the high windows. Various shades of marble statuary filled the center of the room. Carpets were piled against another wall. Against the third wall bronzes of every shape seem tangled in a silent battle. One statue of Minerva gleamed in gold from head to toe. Boxes of silver, ivory, gold, and inlaid woods of various sizes crammed together on a series of shelves.

Sabinus said, "He collected things. He collected people. And, he wanted Philo to be like him, but Philo has a different temperament. As much as he tried to please his father, he couldn't fit the mold. Pius was like a bully. Not that he hit the boy or any member of his family, he did it with words—humiliation, judgments of failure. None of them met his arbitrary standards."

Argolicus pulled his eyes away from the treasures. "You say he collected people. What do you mean?"

"Pius did favors for people and expected something in return. Most of the items here in this room, the other two, at his villa in Ostia, and his home in Rome are gifts. He didn't ask for them directly, but everyone understood that a favor, like the Siren being unloaded today before other ships in the harbor, called for a gift. Things arrive here, 'For his Sublimity the gracious Pius from his grateful friend.' The items went into the warehouse and the note went to Pius."

"But, the people. What do you mean he collected people?"

Nikolaos must have overcome his seasickness, he began scribbling notes.

"I'm not sure how he did it, but he seemed to have a hold on people. For some, he would ask outrageous favors and they were granted without question. If I asked him, he would say, 'You take care of the harbor, I'll manage the politics.' That was as much as he told me. He was my brother, but not my confidant. That's the way he was. He took from people, but he shared nothing unless it was in his interest."

Argolicus thought any of a number of people could have had reason to wish Pius out of their life. From no possibilities, to a large selection, but where would he start? He chewed his lip for a moment and then said, "Your wife wants us to eat the midday meal at your home?"

"Yes," Sabinus said. "We'll get Larcius. It's just a few minutes walk."

"What did you discover?" Philo asked.

"You have a great responsibility ahead of you. Philo, how much did your father tell you about his business connections?"

"Why, do you think one of his connections killed him?"

"It's possible," said Argolicus. "So think. How much do you know about his connections?"

They were in the office at the villa. Philo sat at the desk piled with various stacks of papers. He fanned the edges of one stack, then another, as Argolicus waited for his answer. Philo lifted his head and his eyes brimmed with tears.

"I tried. I tried. But we were so different. I wanted to please my father. He didn't have friends, he had business relationships. I have friends. A few, but friends. Like the ones who would go to the Counselor Games with me. My father brought people here for dinners regularly, but he met with people other places. He didn't take me with him for those. Look at this." He held up a paper from the desk and read, "*Dearest Pius, what you ask is difficult. I thought our arrangement did not include the shipments from Egypt.* I do not understand what that means. How do I answer this?" he looked at the paper, "Caius Hirtius Lucullus. I don't know him."

"You will get in touch with each of them. As they tell you, you will know what to do. You will determine the ones who seek the truth and the ones who hide it. This business is yours now. You don't have to be like your father. Be yourself."

"I don't know how," Philo answered. His face wrenched in anxiety.

"You do. You will discover a way." Argolicus gave him an encouraging smile. Inside he churned with sympathy for the young man who had inherited a corrupt world from his father. He changed the subject, "Any news of the Promag-istrate?"

"No, nothing. Thank you for probing into my father's death. I don't expect you to discover anything, but I appreciate your support."

CHAPTER 5

SISTER IN THE NIGHT

Titiana startled Argolicus as she slipped past a sleeping Nikolaos and stood in the room. His head was bent over his notes on the small table in his room. He had a list of people he knew were involved with Pius. Under each name he jotted what he knew. The girl whispered, "My father was a philanderer of the worst sort."

Argolicus composed himself and asked, "What do you mean?"

"He held orgies." Her voice rose above a whisper.

"Orgies?"

"Yes, all those powerful people, he blackmailed them."

If Nikolaos was awake now, he was keeping quiet.

"Powerful, like Boethius?" Argolicus asked. Boethius might be rich but he also seemed an honest man.

"No, no, no. He didn't go to the parties. It was lesser men. Not consuls and the wealthy but officials—a tax collector, the Promagistrate, military captains, merchants. People like that."

"Titiana, how do you know this?" Argolicus was familiar

with young women and their tendency to exaggerate. And, young people often thought the worst of their parents.

"Pacilus. I've had a crush on him since I was eight. Then we became friends, but not lovers."

Argolicus looked at Titiana's elegant face and wondered if she was lying to preserve her Roman dignity. "Why not lovers?"

Titiana paused. Her face betrayed her effort to solve a dilemma. "It couldn't happen... we were friends... friends. We shared our secrets. He preferred men to women."

"I see. He told you this in friendship?"

"Yes. Don't tell Philo. Don't tell Mother. She would never let me see Pacilus again. She's a prude." Titiana wiped a tear from her cheek, her eyes pleaded with Argolicus. "I think she suspects about the parties, but chooses not to know. Pacilus is my best friend."

Argolicus now understood her hesitancy. "I will tell no one."

He put his hand on her shoulder.

"Tell me about the parties, what Pacilus told you."

"Disgusting... they were disgusting. My father." Titiana swallowed, then took a breath. Her eyes went from Argolicus to Nikolaos' chamber.

"Don't worry about Nikolaos. He is discreet."

"Well," Titiana began. "He... my father... his friends." She stopped. She brought her eyes back to Argolicus. "I don't know where to begin."

"Tell me how Pacilus told you."

"He came here one morning. 'Let's go for a walk,' he said. I knew he wanted to tell me something important. We walk for the big talks."

Titiana held her hands out toward the brazier as if the warmth could help her tell the story.

"We went down by the marshes. No one goes there."

"I was there yesterday."

"So you know how bleak it is. Suddenly Pacilus grabbed my hand. Tears trickled down his cheek. 'Titi,' he said. That's his pet name for me. 'Titi, I need to tell you about your father.' And then it all came out. My father sent him an invitation. Pacilus was excited. He'd heard about gatherings of important men and felt honored to attend a festivity where he could mingle with important people to enhance his career." Her dark lashes glistened with tears for her friend.

"When Pacilus arrived, the luxury awed him and the mix of people impressed him. You've seen my father's study. The party was just as elaborate—food, wine, flowers, party favors. He met many important men and other emerging young men like himself. Good families, but not aristocracy. And beautiful young women he'd never met before."

Titiana took a deep breath.

"And then it changed."

Argolicus dreaded what he knew would come next.

"Men disappeared into other rooms," Titiana continued. "With a girl... or a boy. Pacilus found himself with the Promagistrate's hand on his arm. 'Let's see what you are made of, Pacilus.' Pacilus felt uneasy. He has a lover... several. But the Promagistrate? Pacilus felt nothing but disgust once he realized what his intent was. He said he had to go to the latrines and fled. So, that's what he told me... in confidence." She burst into tears.

"Titiana," Argolicus said. "Was Pacilus angry at your father?"

"How could he not be angry? My father invited him on pretense to use him... as a commodity. Another item for his collection. And then he offered him to anyone. More than anything, Pacilus felt Father had betrayed his trust. Pacilus was ashamed. Ashamed that he had been so trusting and naïve."

She stopped as several emotions crossed her face, sorrow, anger, a slight smile. "I was the one who was angry. My father had done this to my best friend." Frown lines creased her flawless brow. "Before that I considered my father distant. But then, after Pacilus told me, I hated him. I hated him with all my heart. As much as I love Pacilus, I hated my father."

She turned her head and looked in his eyes. Argolicus could see the cold hate.

"Would your friend Pacilus take us to this place?"

"We don't need Pacilus. He showed me where it is. I can take you there."

"Yes, let's go first thing in the morning."

Titiana wiped her eyes and nodded agreement.

"I know where Pater kept his keys. I'll take you."

Argolicus wanted more information. Any evil, like decadence, was bound to cause resentment. "Now, tell me more about the men who were there. Did they pay Pius to organize these parties? Or, did they all contribute?"

Titiana opened her eyes wide. "My father did not discuss these matters with me. He kept these activities hidden from the women of the house. Pacilus wouldn't know, either. My father's good name duped him to attend. That invitation..." She shook her head.

"Here's one thing I know. My father liked to own people. He liked to have something on them, have a hold on them. Control, that's what he wanted. As pater familias he ruled our family. Mother came to terms with him. Her life was here but mostly separate. Philo suffered the most with his sensitive and scholarly nature. Pater did not appreciate those qualities. He belittled Philo. I would do anything for my brother. He is sweet and kind..."

"Titiana, tell me anything you know about the parties.

Anything that Pacilus told you. In my short time here I have a sense of how your father treated his family, all of it. I spent time with Sabinus, his brother. I saw your father's storerooms. Your uncle hinted at the control your father had over the business. Unless you think a member of your family killed your father, I want to consider who would hate your father so much. Who would carry hate in his or her heart strong enough to stab him like that, with force and violence?"

Titiana shook her head again. "No. No one in the family. I can't believe anyone in the family carries that much hate. Look at my cousin Larcius, so methodical. And Uncle Sabinus he's..."

Argolicus was liking this young woman. Her love of her family and her forthright honesty. But her youthful babbling was preventing him from getting to the point, the real killer of her father. He mustered his patience and said, "Titiana, the parties. Who was at the parties? Of the men Pacilus mentioned can you think of anyone?"

"I don't know. I know Father had a hold on all of them. I'm a girl. I meet those men on formal occasions..."

"Could you make a list of the men that Pacilus told you were there? That would help me. Unless I knew them in Rome, I wouldn't know the local patricians."

"Oh, yes. I could do that. I'll have it for you in the morning."

As soon as she left, Nikolaos ducked into the room from his alcove. "A despicable man."

"So it seems," Argolicus replied. "I don't know how I will come to any resolution before we leave for home. I'm not sure if going to this hall will help in any way. It will be empty. It's the people I need to know. I don't see how we'll meet those bureaucrats and minor officials that attended those parties in the little time we have left."

"His hidden life," Nikolaos prompted.

"Yes, the people in his hidden life. Even if the girl gives us a list, how can we meet them all and discover anything of depth in one day. It seems impossible. At this point it seems the best I can do is leave my notes with Philo to give to the Promagistrate when he returns. And, even then, he has total discretion over whether he wants to investigate the killing or leave it to the family. It's a matter of how the Promagistrate interprets his death as impacting the public good."

Argolicus sat in thought. His head swirled with questions without answers. Who were the men? Which one hated Pius the most? How could he discover that? The person who hated him the most might be the best at covering up his feelings.

Nikolaos interrupted his thoughts. "Pius was the most important man in Ostia. Wouldn't that make it a circum-stance of public good?"

"Not necessarily. The business will continue with Sabinus and the commerce is the public good. Plus, the business is across the Tiber in Portus, not Ostia."

"Young Ma... Master," Nikolaos corrected himself. "That puts us in a tight situation. One day. One day."

"Yes, right now it seems impossible. Perhaps Titiana's list will help. She's an aware young woman. She can tell us about the people on her list."

"Still, one day is a short time. You must put that mind of yours to work."

Argolicus chuckled. "Your opinion of me is higher than I deserve. Titiana's faith in her family is tender but I'm not yet ruling out the family. Perhaps Philo knew more about his father than his sister thinks. He has reason to resent his father. But hate, I don't see hate. And, Aemilia keeps closed. She is just the type of person I thought of when hate runs deep but is covered by reserve."

Nikolaos said, "But, you should examine that more. She is

resistant to your looking into the death of her husband. Isn't that suspicious?"

The lamp on the table flickered. The painted figures on the wall seemed to dance but Argolicus felt as though they were mocking his inadequacy.

"This all started with politics and favors. Boethius is a powerful man. It seemed like a simple gesture at the time. One last gesture to the citizens of Rome as I left for home. Deliver a book to a young scholar. Now I've given my word and will fail Philo at a vulnerable time." He slumped in his seat and stared at his notes.

"Master, Philo understands that you did this out of consideration."

"I know how devastated I felt when my father died. He wasn't murdered. It was a freak accident. I can't imagine how murder would affect a young man, a very violent murder."

"Then let's focus on what we can do," practical Nikolaos replied, urging on his master.

Argolicus looked up. "Think of those stab wounds. Deep and multiple. Perhaps, but unlikely. Sabinus could travel back and forth on his vessel and would have access to the villa. We spent the day with him and he seems to understand his brother's failings, tolerates them, and concentrates on the business."

Nikolaos shook his head. "No, but what about the boys? Not Titiana's friend, but one of the other boys. Is it possible that another boy did not escape the way Titiana's friend did and now harbors guilt and shame?"

"That is a consideration," Argolicus replied. He mulled on this for a moment in silence. "That is a very strong consideration. A young man, strong and harboring revenge. Someone like that could have stabbed in a rage. But how would they get in the house in the early morning?"

They both sat in silence. Argolicus yawned and said, "I thought a friend of Philo's might have got him to open the side door, but then Philo would be awake and wouldn't leave him alone with Pius. No, that makes little sense. It's time to sleep. Perhaps we will wake up with fresh insights."

CHAPTER 6
SEDUCTION AND POWER

In the early morning, Philo discovered them all—Argolicus, Nikolaos, Titiana, and her friend Pacilus—getting ready to leave.

"Pacilus! What are you doing here? Where are you all going?" Philo asked.

Pacilus, a handsome, well-built young man with dark curls and seductive brown eyes fringed with long, dark lashes, stood mute.

Titiana lowered her gaze and then answered before Pacilus could say a word, "Philo, there are aspects of Pater that you don't know."

"What? What are they? Is this about his murder? Where are you going?" Dark circles under his eyes revealed his sleepless night.

Argolicus stepped up to answer. "Philo, your father was not as noble as he first appeared. Pacilus discovered something... dark about your father. We will investigate. One of the unpleasant consequences of a killing is that hidden facts come to light."

"What facts?" Philo asked. "Where are you going? Who...?"

"We don't know all the facts, yet," Argolicus answered. "That's why we will examine one of his holdings here in Ostia, a place where he held... gatherings. Parties for certain men."

"Certain men? That doesn't sound factual to me. What parties?"

"Parties for men only," Argolicus said. "And young men like Pacilus."

Philo turned to Pacilus. "You attended these parties?"

Pacilus, looking uncomfortable, nodded. "Once."

Titiana turned to her brother. "Philo. It is time for you to be an adult. I know how Pater treated you. It wasn't just you. He manipulated many people. Come with us. Discover a facet of your father he kept from all of us. Then you will have a new fact."

Philo had the look of a wounded pigeon. He stood still his eyes focused on some internal vision none of them could see. "I'll come."

Pacilus led them through the streets to an old building that had once been shops but now appeared closed along with several others along the street. Set on the main street, Decumanus Maximus, the building looked as deserted as so many buildings in Ostia. "This is it," he said.

Titiana crossed to the main door and inserted a large iron key. She turned the lock, and the door opened.

Their eyes became accustomed to the dark room lit only by the high windows beside the main door. The plastered walls were painted with figures of men embracing in a variety of positions—standing, sitting, sprawled on beds. Faint scents of perfume, burnt oil, and spices lingered in the air.

Pacilus gestured with his arm. "This is the main reception.

The private rooms are behind, and there's a door beyond that leads to baths. Everything I saw here..." He stopped unable to describe his experience.

Philo asked, "What happened here? I don't understand."

Titiana said, "Philo, take a look at the paintings. Our father held parties here... for men. And for young men. He used his influence to invite young men like Pacilus. Pacilus came expecting honor among men of power in a congenial atmosphere. Instead, it was an invitation to seduction."

Pacilus added, "Philo, there's something you should know about me."

Philo said, "I know. You've been a friend of Titiana's since childhood. I'm not *that* naïve. I saw the signs. You never wanted Titiana. Look at her. She is beautiful. You think I didn't know."

Titiana gave him a hug. "Oh, Philo. You are so discreet. You understand. Pacilus is my best friend. Most girls have best friends that are girls, but Pacilus is mine. I can tell him anything."

Philo said, "You are lucky. I have friends, but no best friend. I wanted to go to the Games with others who were going, but not anyone as a friend. Just company. I thought Father would feel secure that I was with others."

Argolicus brought them back to the reason for the visit, "Pacilus, tell us what happened when you arrived."

Pacilus blushed. "I... I... I was so hopeful when I arrived. A doorman asked to see my invitation. I entered expecting to hobnob with the local elite. I was—I still am—looking to advance my political career. I want to leave Ostia and to end up in Rome."

Argolicus nodded commiserating with the young man's ambition. At the same time, he wanted to go home more than ever to escape the Roman clambering for position.

"He's so good with people. They talk to him," Titiana volunteered.

"Go on," Argolicus prompted. "What happened once you were past the doorman?"

"It was nothing like it looks now. There were lamps and lanterns everywhere. The room was bright with flickering light. *Gustum* delicacies filled the tables. A fountain of honeyed wine sat in the middle of one table and slaves circulated with pitchers to fill goblets. Men, and the guests were all men, dressed in finery. Scents from perfumed oils and pomades saturated the air." He paused and took a breath, glancing at Argolicus.

Argolicus said, "I realize how difficult it is to remember and tell us. Any details will help. Did you recognize anyone?"

"Yes," Pacilus said. "Most of the men. They were major citizens here in Ostia or in Rome, but here in Ostia for the time."

"Can you add to the list Titiana made?" He reached toward Nikolaos who brought out a small parchment from somewhere in his folds.

"I'll write them down," Pacilus said, as he took the sheet from Nikolaos. "There were a few girls, prostitutes, too. But I don't know their names."

"The girls aren't important. Whoever you remember," Argolicus said. "What about the other young men?"

"I recognized most of them. Some could have been in one of the... other rooms. The private rooms. The rooms where... things happened. Not that they were friends. Ostia is a small town and even smaller when you consider the patricians, most of whom visit from Rome. Pater was one of the few who lived here most of the time. There was Nobilier, he's the son of a military naval officer, and Macrinus—I'm uncertain what his father does—and Arsenius, the son of the Promagistrate, and Otho. His father is a prominent silk merchant."

"Did you talk to any of them? Had any of them been to other parties?"

"I don't know," Pacilus said. "If they had, they probably thought, as I thought at the beginning, that the parties were a step to position and power."

Philo interrupted. "My father! My father did this? Why did everyone know but me?"

Titiana hugged her brother close. "Philo, these are the facts. We have to learn them and know who our father was. You can go home."

"No, I'm staying. Show me the list. Now that father is gone, I need to know who took part in these scandalous activities. Knowledge is power just as much as wealth. I will have nothing to do with them."

"Philo, it's not that easy. You are right," Argolicus said. "Knowledge is power. At times, especially in politics—and a small town is almost nothing but politics—that knowledge gives you the advantage. You know of a weakness that those men think is a secret. That knowledge gives you the strength to work with them, to converse, to transact business, to see them in normal social settings. Your anger now may keep you from wanting to see them, but you will soon discover that situations arise when it is better to consider them, to attend to them rather than avoid them. Anything you do here will train you for coping with Rome itself."

"Well, you may be right. But now I am angry." Philo's face flushed and his fists balled at the end of his slender arms.

Once again, Argolicus' heart went out to the boy. His own introduction to the adult world of complexities after his own father's death was similar, but without the grim veneer of murder. "The world of adults is complicated. And politics compounds the difficulties. It's why I'm leaving Rome. I understand. The complications are wearing. I'm going home to avoid those complications."

Philo gave him a grateful look and his face changed to thoughtfulness. "That's just the problem. You can go home to the south far away from Rome and politics, but I'm here in Ostia with Rome just a few miles away. I have no escape."

Titiana grabbed his hand and squeezed. "Philo, I know you will be a leader. Not in the way father was by manipulating people, but in *your* way. You've inherited Pater's wealth, but not his way of doing things."

Argolicus said, "Wise words from your sister. Now, let's hear more from Pacilus."

Pacilus looked around. "I was at a table piled with snacks talking to a man from Rome, I don't remember his name, when Numerius Sulpicius Asina joined us. The Roman left. That's when..." Pacilus hesitated. He looked at Titiana who nodded. "That's when Asina put his hand on my arm. He stroked it and said, 'Let's see what you are made of.' That's when I understood the party was not what I thought. He was inviting me to go to one of those rooms." He gestured to the doorway on the far side of the hall. "I couldn't. I just couldn't. I excused myself to the latrines in the middle of the building and then left by a side door."

He looked down at the parchment in his hand.

"These men," he continued, waving the list. "These men are not about affection. They are about power over other people." He looked down at the list. "Almost all of them are married and have families. It's not about sexual preference. They want the power of seduction and the influence of secrets. Yes. As humiliated as I was, I'm glad I left. Argolicus, if there's a way I can help you find Pius' murderer, I will. Titiana and Philo deserve to know."

"You are helping now," Argolicus said. "I have today, and then I'm gone. Not everyone would do what you've done—swallow their pride to come here with us. The ordinary exterior appearing as abandoned shops tells me how Pius wanted to keep these parties a secret. Our next step is to examine the list. Add any names you remember to the list. Then, if you want to help more, any of you, help me with reasons any of these men would want to kill Pius."

All three of the young people agreed.

"We've seen enough here. Let's go back to Philo's *domus* and study the list."

☙❧

PHILO AND TITIANA LEFT TO HELP AEMILIA WITH FUNERAL arrangements. Pacilus added in two names on the list and left for home. Argolicus sat in his makeshift study at the small table in his guest room as he reviewed the list.

Between Titiana and Pacilus there were twelve names in total on the parchment scrap. Twelve names. Twelve men he didn't know. In an unfamiliar town.

He grabbed the parchment, stood up and called, "Nikolaos, quick. Catch Pacilus before he leaves the *domus*. We need him. I'll be downstairs in the *peristylum*."

When Pacilus arrived in a few minutes, Argolicus said, "I need your help again. If we go to the forum, most of the men on the list will be there. It's morning. Everyone is out conducting business, gossiping, and just being seen. I'm sure it's the same here as the forum in any town."

"That's what it's like this time of day," Pacilus said. "What do you need from me?"

"I need your help to match names to faces. If you could point out the people on the list—discreetly—I'll have a better idea of who they are. Can you help?"

"Of course," Pacilus said. "Any way I can help Titiana and Philo, I am ready."

Argolicus led them into the office where Philo, Titiana, Aemilia, and Sabinus gathered around the large table. The table was clear of trinkets as they four of them pored over papers. Old Ioses and Philo's tutor Bion sat at one end of the table writing invitations to the funeral in elegant cursive.

"I'm off to the forum with Pacilus," Argolicus said.

CHAPTER 7
NOT THE MAN

The bright morning sun did little to ease the crisp air, but it brought what people were in Ostia to the forum. Wrapped in heavy cloaks over layers of clothing tradesmen hawked their wares beside empty stalls, barbers busied themselves with blades, and the patricians and politicians stood in groups in the center of the large plaza chatting and exchanging gossip. The empty shops marked only by the mosaic emblems set in the stones in front showed how much the town had dwindled to serve only the few patricians who still came to their country retreats.

They passed groups of people and overheard snippets of conversation. *Ostia will not be the same. A vicious murder I hear. Young Philo...* Talk of Pius' murder was the main topic of conversation.

Argolicus knew he had made the right decision when he noticed the clusters of men talking in the large plaza. He turned to Pacilus.

"If you see any of those men on the list, point them out discreetly. Tell me his name. Mention his position and anything else you know about him. Nikolaos will take notes."

"How will that help?" Pacilus asked.

"I want to know them better. I want a sense of who they are and how they conduct themselves in public." He pulled his cloak tighter as a quick gust came off the ocean. "Is it always this cold here?"

Pacilus laughed. "In the winter." Then his look sobered.

"And there you see," he gestured with his shoulder toward three men chatting, "in that group is one Numerius Mummius Paterculus. He has holdings here and a large family villa. He is often in Rome but here in Ostia enough, enough to be part of Pius' circle."

Nikolaos scribbled on the list.

"I recognize him from Rome," Argolicus said. "He loves gossip of any kind."

Before Argolicus could move toward the group Paterculus called, "Your Sublimity, here you are in Ostia. Come, come. Join us." He was a thin man with a rapacious look to his otherwise bland face.

Argolicus joined the group, introduced Pacilus, and met the other two men.

"Tell us, Argolicus, what brings you to Ostia. Are you avoiding the *hoi polloi* and madness of the Games as we are? Flavius Paulus is a good man, God bless him." He crossed himself quickly but without reverence. "But you know how it is. He isn't as rich as some, and I understand the Games are not as lavish this year...

"I am returning home to Bruttia tomorrow."

A brief disdainful sneer crossed Paterculus' face before he returned to his mask of avid interest.

Argolicus continued, "On my way, I did a favor for Boethius. And now I'm doing a favor for young Servius Norbanus Philo."

"Oh, I heard. I heard." Paterculus said, crossing himself

three times as did his two companions. "Such a horror. Who would think it? How fortunate for Philo that you are a magistrate. I remember how you settled that dispute with Velusian's sons. Something about the circus tower and the amphitheater." He paused hoping Argolicus would fall for the bait and explain.

Argolicus remembered the sons Marcian and Maximiums, how they had lost those items in a drunken gamble to him. He thought of that incident as his true entry into the adult world. The debt was not recorded. Argolicus had trusted their word, and the sons had petitioned King Theodoric to reclaim their ownership. The matter would haunt him for life. "I'm retiring from the Senate and returning home. Our ship leaves tomorrow. I'm not certain I can help Philo much in the time I'm here."

"Well, you can leave in peace. I hear Numerius Sulpicius Asina returns tomorrow. Although..."

"Yes, it is a family matter," Argolicus said, reading Paterculus' thoughts. He decided to plumb the meddler's knowledge. "Would he help the family even though it's not a public matter?"

"Oh, I know him well. In this case, he might. He and Pius were good friends."

"That's good to hear. Philo and the family will receive support. The murder was quite violent."

Paterculus was all ears, ready for details, but Argolicus cut off his prurient pursuit. "I'm off to find some good vellum to take on my trip. It was good to see you again and meet your friends." He nodded to the three and walked on, Pacilus at his side and Nikolaos trailing behind.

Pacilus said, "What a man," as his eyes followed Paterculus. "I wonder how I can navigate gossips like that. You do it so well."

"I'm not so sure," Argolicus said. "I find gossips trying. If you learn to observe and curb your responses, it gets easier. Do you see anyone else on the list?"

Pacilus shook his head no.

"Master, now that you mention it," Nikolaos said, "more vellum at cheap prices is a good idea to take back to the country."

"We'll do that," Argolicus responded. "First, let's see who else Pacilus knows so he can have the rest of the day to himself."

"Do you see those two men next to the big well? They are both on the list, I saw them that night," Pacilus said. "Pansa and Rufus. Publius Hirtius Pansa and Servius Marius Rufus. Pansa's family has been in Ostia for generations. He owns property here and in Portus. He was often at Philo's *domus*. I saw him on my visits with Titiana."

Pansa was a big man, but it was difficult to tell how big because he was swathed in layers of bright silks—blue, green, red, and yellow—topped by a heavy fur against the chill. On his feet he wore court style, heavily embroidered soft shoes with crossed straps over the instep. The other man, Rufus, wore a embroidered tunic covered by a wool cape and sturdier shoes with wrappings up to his knees against the cold.

"Rufus is another who lives in Rome but comes to a family villa here in Ostia," Pacilus said. "I know little about him because he's mostly in Rome."

Argolicus lowered his head, wondering how he would greet them without seeming obvious. He strolled among the crowds and this time heard snatches of conversation about himself. *Praetor and then praefect of the city... He must be a friend of the family, I've never seen him here in Ostia... Is he leaving in disgrace...? Those young sycophants of the King...*

His dilemma resolved when Rufus called out as they neared the central well. "Your Sublimity, I see you, too, are avoiding the Games. We are honored to see you in Ostia."

Argolicus approached shaking his head, "No, I'm going home. I've left the public world."

"But I hear you are helping the family of Servius Norbanus Pius," Pansa said, pulling his fur over the silk layers.

"I am. I was there hours after it happened on an errand for Boethius, and Philo asked for my help when I delivered Boethius' gift, a book."

Pansa continued, "Pius was such an important man here. So many of us respected him. Young Philo must be devastated. Book, you say. You brought a book?"

"Yes, one Boethius wrote himself."

Both men looked at him again. He could see their reappraisal at the mention of Boethius, one of the richest men in Rome. Argolicus had a sense of why they had come under Pius' sway. Riches impressed them.

"Yes, well... an outsider wouldn't be able to help much, but it is a cordial gesture," Rufus said. "Murders are so difficult to trace if done in private. I suppose the family has no recourse but to depend on a kind gesture from someone like you. A man from the provinces. And I hear your mother is one of the King's People. Your father..." He left the sentence unfinished.

Argolicus heard the intended slur and ignored it. He was here to discover what he could about these men. He saw Pansa give Rufus a warning glance. Argolicus felt Pacilus tense.

"Rome has changed," Pansa said, bringing neutrality to the conversation. "We have a King in Ravenna and are left to ourselves here. He doesn't visit Rome. I've been to Ravenna several times. It's full of pomp and regal splendor. The entire palace is a copy of the palace in Constantinople. We Romans have to acknowledge that Rome is not Rome. The Emperor is in Constantinople and the King is in Ravenna. Most of the goods that pass through Portus go to Ravenna and the north, not Rome. I've heard the great orator Cassiodorus. Isn't he a friend of yours?"

"He is," said Argolicus. "A gifted speaker. We're childhood friends."

Rufus said under his breath, "Aha."

Pansa went on ignoring Rufus. "His laws are fair. He's left Roman law in place for citizens. That doesn't help Pius' family though. The King's People, have a penalty for killing. Even though it is money or something else of value, we Roman citizens must deal with killings on our own. I've heard of your decisions. Often just and usually fair. If you find the killer, I know your recommendations to the family will be honorable."

"Thank you," Argolicus said. "I wonder if you could help me? Do you know anyone who held a grudge against Pius? Any unfair dealings?"

"He was a rich man involved in many transactions," Pansa said. "Too many for me to know. I'm afraid I knew him only as a patrician. I've heard no grumbling about his business dealings."

"He exacted full... he traded in favors," Rufus said. "I won't deny it. In personal business he's not the man many admire. In business there was always a personal favor as well as the transaction. Some became uneasy with his favors. Pius always seemed to come out ahead. But grumbling is not a cause for murder."

He had touched on the truth about Pius.

Argolicus agreed. "You are right. Being disgruntled does not lead to murder. Can you think of anyone who had a more powerful resentment?"

Both men shook their heads. Rufus looked up and glanced at Pacilus. "I know you. You're Lucius Mummius Pacilus, yes? You are a friend of the daughter, Titiana. I feel as though we've met."

Pacilus shook his head as his body tensed. "No. I mean, yes, I am a friend of the family. But, as far as I know, we haven't met."

Argolicus knew it was time to go. Pacilus was fragile about the party. Much more prying and the young man might fall into tears or break down in some other way.

"You've been helpful," he said to the two men. "I'm staying at the family villa. If you think of something, anything that might help, send a message. I can meet with you. A visit to the household now is not right. The entire family is distraught."

Argolicus left the two patricians of Ostia and walked toward the market stalls that surrounded the large plaza. Pacilus was silent, lost in his thoughts.

"Pacilus, do you see any more of the men on that list?" Argolicus asked.

Pacilus lifted his head and glanced around the plaza. "No. The others may have gone to Rome for the Counselor Games or they're just not here today." He turned his head to look at Argolicus. "I need to leave. That meeting with Pansa. I was at that party such a short time. He recognized my face."

"Pacilus, you did nothing at that event. You left before anything happened. We all have a moment when we leave the naïvete of youth. Yours was quick with no real dire consequences." He thought about the Roman brothers and their gambling trick. "Mine came much later. Many would have called me a man at twenty-eight, but in some ways I was more naïve than you. And I had unpleasant consequences. Friends like Philo and Titiana support you. You have the rest of your life. You handled that brief situation well. And, you were right. You hadn't met Pansa. It's just that you saw him at the party."

"You think I handled myself well?"

"Yes. Yes, I do. You will serve your ambition to be in politics. It takes practice. That was practice."

Pacilus smiled. Argolicus nodded and returned the smile.

"Thank you for your help, Pacilus. Nikolaos, let's find that vellum."

CHAPTER 8
THE PRICE OF NOBILITY

Nikolaos clutched the wrapped pack of vellum sheets under his arm. Argolicus strode in thought along the main road of Ostia, Decumanus Maximus. When the road angled toward the town wall, he continued walking headed for the main gate and the shore of the ocean. They passed the baths and the guild house and working people on the street who served the needs of the lingering patricians. Argolicus was the only patrician on the street as they walked between shops, workshops, bars, and restaurants, interspersed by empty buildings, toward the city gate.

Argolicus spoke. "There was snow in Rome but it seems colder here, even with the sun almost at midday."

"No complaining," Nikolaos chided.

"I'm stating a fact. I feel as though it's the only fact I know at the moment. My head is swimming with possibilities about Pius, his family, and his cohorts." He stopped walking and tradesmen, slaves, workers flowed around him some giving a fleeting look at his finery, others ignoring the patrician and his slave.

"Master, would you like to stop at a restaurant for a light meal? Perhaps that would clear your head."

Argolicus glanced at the street ahead. Small bars and restaurants sat between shops at regular intervals. "A good idea."

"That one looks quiet," Nikolaos said pointing to an open door ahead.

Argolicus nodded. They found a table inside, and he said, "Whatever looks good."

He sat while Nikolaos left to place an order. A young peasant couple sat at a corner table gazing into each other's eyes. Four workers chatted amiably before the midday break. The rest of the room sat in empty gloom. He mulled over his lack of progress. His offer of help to Philo was coming to no conclusion. He had a better picture of Pius and his manipulations but had met no one who seemed angry enough for a vicious attack in the man's own home. How had they made it inside? It had to be the side door. The big doorkeeper would have known any other entrance.

Nikolaos returned and placed flatbread, an egg, a bowl of steaming lamb stew, and a cup of wine in front of Argolicus.

"I keep thinking it was someone Pius knew well," Argolicus said. "Otherwise, they would not have access to the house, even the side entrance. The slaves coming and going would have noticed. Aemilia is cold and bitter, but she seems resigned and not angry. Titiana hated her father. But those stab wounds, I don't see her doing that."

"What about Pacilus?" Nikolaos ventured. "We have only Titiana's word that he was more wounded than angry."

"We spent the morning with him. He's more worried about how to pursue a career than hatred. After all, nothing happened. I don't see him like that, full of vengeful anger. I thought about him briefly when Titiana visited, but spending the morning with him, no."

He dipped a piece of flatbread in the stew.

"And those men at the forum. Whatever hold Pius had on them, they were all sycophants at heart. Pansa with his courtier ways without a court. Rufus with his disdain, ready to belittle anyone. Paterculus and his gossip-mongering. None of them particularly admirable men."

The tangy odors of the stew made Argolicus realize he was hungry. He ate in earnest. As he savored the stew and rich spices he tempered the spices with pieces of bread and went back over the morning. The visit to the party site, the people Pacilus had seen there, Philo's shock, the conversations in the forum. Nothing stood out. He was overlooking something important someone had said but did not understand what it was.

"Could it be one of the other boys?" Nikolaos asked. He pulled out a note and glanced at it. "Nobilier - naval officer. Macrinus - unknown. Arsenius - Promagistrate. Otho - silk merchant. Perhaps one of them was actually seduced. Didn't escape like Pacilus. And afterward blamed Pius and his decadent gatherings."

"The boys," Argolicus said, slapping his palm on the table. "I knew there was something I overlooked. Exactly, possibly one of them or another young man from another party at another time. A 17- or 18-year-old would have plenty of strength. Even a younger boy who was strong. Let's go back to the villa. Perhaps Philo can help us, at least with these boys."

Nikolaos put away his note and reached for the package of vellum sheets.

Argolicus took a last gulp of wine from the cup, then stood. When he looked around the bar, he noticed the room was empty. The barman stood in the back while voices and clattering came from the kitchen, but the room itself was empty.

A silhouette stood in the doorway backlit by the winter sun. A large man entered the relative dark. Tall, but not as tall as Argolicus, dressed in a shabby tunic covered on top by a short leather tunic with no sleeves. A wide leather belt left over from some military campaign circled his waist.

The man strode to Argolicus and whispered in a rough hiss, "Do not meddle." He reached out his hardened fingers and clutched the front of Argolicus' tunic. He pulled Argolicus toward him so that his stinking breath flooded the close air. "You are out of your element. The price of nobility is birth right. You are only half there."

Argolicus tensed and growled. "I have a trusted mission. I keep my word."

The man pushed his hand against Argolicus' chest with vigor, let go of his tunic, and turned toward the door. "As do I," he said, striding toward the doorway where he hovered for a moment and then disappeared into the sunlight.

Nikolaos sighed and said, "Master, why did you not fight back?"

"The man was rough, but no threat. He meant no physical harm. The words were a threat." He smoothed the front of his tunic with his palm. "But he was a messenger, not the man or woman who sent the threat."

"Your questions and explorations have unsettled someone."

"Now we need to find out who that is."

When Argolicus and Nikolaos returned, the giant doorman N'Golo leaned close to Argolicus and said, "I think Philo will be glad you are here. They are all in the entertainment room."

From the *atrium,* Argolicus could hear the voices. Among

them, he heard Philo and Aemilia arguing with someone. Argolicus headed toward the large room behind the *peristylum* while Nikolaos went up to the room to store the vellum package.

In the elegant room, the braziers burned hot with coals but there was no food. Philo, Titiana, Aemilia, and Sabinus sat while a large man, dressed in silks in much the same manner as Pansa down to the embroidered soft black shoes stood gesticulating. His brown hair was smoothed down over the crown with scented pomade. Heavy, dark eyebrows arched over deep brown eyes. He strode with a commanding bearing as he addressed the family, "... because my hands are tied. It's outside the law..."

"Argolicus," Philo said, jumping up, a look of relief on his face. "This is the Promagistrate Numerius Sulpicius Asina."

Asina turned toward Argolicus, "Your Sublimity, as you know, this killing, vicious as it may be, is a family matter. There's no way I can help the family of Servius Norbanus Pius. He was a friend. But, from a legal standpoint, there is nothing I can do. His death is not a public matter."

Argolicus would have to wait to tell Philo about the ruffian or ask him about the boys on the list. He chest ached where the man had pushed him.

Titiana noticed his rumpled appearance and raised an eyebrow.

He gave her a slight nod and turned toward Asina. "Promagistrate, I explained the legalities to Philo when I arrived. The family has money to take up a suit in a court of law, but first, we must find the killer."

"Exactly what I was explaining to them," Asina said. "It is a family matter, they must find the killer to bring suit."

Argolicus nodded and then asked, "Perhaps one or two of your men might like to take on a special investigation. I'm sure the family would pay well. Men with families who might want to earn extra money. You could give them a leave. Is that a possibility?"

Asina rustled his silks and took a step backward. He pressed his lips together, paused as if thinking, and said, "These men are trained to quell disputes on the street and other disruptions of public order. They are not in any way investigators experienced in finding murderers. The family would not only be wasting money, they would have no satisfaction."

Asina held fast to his legal point, and Argolicus wondered why he would not want to find the man who killed his friend Pius. "I see. Is there a man for hire who would do this? Help a family with private matters?"

"Families. My wife died, I have only my son," Asina deflected, then continued with a noncommittal answer. "I will ask around. Perhaps I can find someone."

"Let me show you the body," Argolicus said, gesturing across the *peristylum* toward the room off the *atrium*. "When you see the wounds, you'll understand how this murder was so vicious. We'll leave the family in peace."

Asina hesitated, then stepped toward Argolicus and followed him toward the *cubiculum*. Nikolaos had returned from their sleeping quarters and trailed behind. When they entered the room Pius was dressed in fine silks. The sweet scent of the pungent oils the slaves had used to clean the body mixed with a slight odor of decay.

Argolicus told a woman sitting in attendance what they needed to see. She shrugged and lifted the silks to expose the wounds. The wounds had turned dark and glistened with the scented oil.

Asina said, "Like battle wounds," as he gazed at Pius' greenish tinged abdomen and the dark maroon stab wounds.

Argolicus said. "A strong arm and great force like the fury of battle. In this case, it was anger. You can see why the entire family is upset and wants to find the murderer. Is there any way you could help his family? I leave tomorrow. I promised Philo I would help, but I have discovered nothing. The more I explore, the wider the circle of possibilities."

"I know Pius and his family. We connected often. I suppose most people would call us friends. I'd like to help, but I can't do anything official."

Argolicus said, "That would relieve my obligation. Philo is a friend of Boethius. They exchanged letters. I came here to deliver a book as a favor and this," he gestured toward Pius' body which was covered again. The old woman adjusted folds in the fabric. "The family leaves tomorrow for the funeral in Rome. I wanted you to see the wounds so you would understand how agitated the killer must have been."

"I'll find someone," Asina said. "I'll talk now to Aemilia to reassure her. I'll explain that I can help, but unofficially." He headed toward the door.

"I will tell Philo," Argolicus said as they left the *cubiculum*.

He found Philo and his uncle sitting in the office. The big table was now covered with account books and each of them was poring over one large tome.

"Philo," Argolicus said standing over the large table. "Asina has agreed to find someone to continue the search. Not a legal search, but a private individual. In some ways, this will be more helpful than anything I could do. A local man will know more about Pius' connections than I do."

"Thank you," Sabinus said. "I don't know why he was being so difficult."

"It was a point of law," Argolicus answered. "Under the law, the matter belongs to the family. Once your brother's killer is found, then it is up to you to bring it to court. I know this is difficult with his death and the funeral arrangements. But now, you will have someone, perhaps two people, to help you find the killer."

Philo looked up at Argolicus. "Thank you. I was thinking like a child when I asked you to help. I have so much to learn. I've decided I want to be more like you, patient and thorough."

Argolicus laughed and said, "Philo, it's as I said when we were out this morning, the more you focus on facts, the better you can facilitate your course with other people. I'm flattered and thank you for the compliment, but it's more a matter of experience in life than any special skills."

Philo nodded. "I do. I have much to face. In that way, maybe Pater was right. I need to socialize with others."

"About your father's death, I have no clues. The circle of people keeps widening rather than narrowing. I'm wondering if you could tell me about the boys Pacilus mentioned." He gestured to Nikolaos who pulled the list out of his folds, walked over from the corner where he'd been standing, and handed it to Argolicus.

"And, I want to tell you about an incident we had after we left Pacilus," Argolicus said.

CHAPTER 9
THE CAUTION

Before Argolicus could begin, Aemilia interrupted crossing the *atrium* from the *cubiculum* containing Pius' remains. Her bearing was as stately as the first day, and her *tunica* a fine green embroidered with gold, but her face was haggard.

"Come," she said gesturing to another *cubiculum* off the *atrium*.

Argolicus brushed at his tunic where the ruffian had clutched and crumpled the fabric, nodded and followed Aemilia through the door. He signaled to Philo that he would return. The boy looked disappointed but nodded. His mother took precedence.

Vivid frescos of pastoral scenes with shepherds, sheep, flowers, and trees covered the painted walls. The mosaic floor echoed the theme in flowers set among diagonal patterns in hues of green, gold, and a soft rose. Two benches with tapestry padded cushions faced each other set for conversation. In the far corner a chair and writing table were arranged, the table top clear except for a sheet of vellum, a pen, and a pot of ink.

"My work room," Aemilia said as she sat with an erect posture on a bench. She gestured to the other bench and nodded to Argolicus to sit. Argolicus mimicked her posture and realized how uncomfortable the backless bench was.

Aemilia folded her hands in her lap. "I hear you are disturbing things. Your visit to the forum is already gossip everywhere. I don't know how to say this, but you must be more discreet. Your direct and forward manner—I know you want to get to the root of things in a short time—but, your manner has disturbed some important people."

"I feel the pressure to find Pius' killer. I have until tomorrow morning. It's seeming that the more I search, the wider the circle of prospects grows." He stopped, considered her words and continued. "You may be right. In my time as *praefectus urbanus* in Rome, I grew accustomed to assuming authority. Here, I am another citizen and have no special authority to question much less probe."

"Pius, whatever he may have been to his family, was a leader, perhaps the most prominent man in Ostia. Unlike most of the patricians, he lived here. The others maintain their places as villas away from the city. They are Romans from Rome. They consider themselves the elite of the elite. But in Ostia, Pius was the lion. Because of his position and his manner, he ran this town. I have my reputation as his wife."

Argolicus mused on the decaying and almost empty Ostia. "I understand. Could you help me? I know I asked before, but now you've had time to reflect. Can you think of anyone, young or old, male or female, wealthy or otherwise, who would have reason to be angry, very angry, with Pius?"

"You've been out. You've seen this once thriving port. Pius was just another patrician in Rome, but here he was the leading man. He was one of few who lived here most of the year. Romans who still visit their villas here, bring their household from Rome. They don't keep a separate staff here. This is a town of ghosts and has beens. If someone was angry enough to confront him face-to-face and kill him, it would be someone who does business here—and, if so, they did business with Pius. Kill? I don't know."

"You knew your husband. Did he...Was he...?"

"Did my husband keep other women? Not that I know, and I would have known. Years ago he thought he fell in love with someone, but she turned out to like his wealth more than him. I think that was a lesson he did not forget. I suppose it is possible that some woman killed him out of jealousy, but I find that very, very difficult to believe. He didn't like encumbrances. That included liaisons that required some form of loyalty. No, I don't see it."

"Did he cheat someone out of money or goods?"

"He didn't cheat. He extracted favors. He held power over people with knowledge. If someone asked him to cheat, that was a thing he knew. He wielded that knowledge to gain favors. A very different way of interacting with people than direct deceit in a business transaction. He brought no one to financial ruin. That wasn't his way. The way he worked was indirect, subtle, and always about power."

Aemilia shifted on the bench and leaned forward, her silks rustling with her movement.

"Whatever motivated someone into anger, it was about power, power over someone. It wasn't about business. It was some way Pius cornered someone with his manipulation. I don't know how you will find that person but that's what I can tell you. It's about power over someone."

Argolicus nodded in agreement. "You and your family have been gracious in hosting me here. I leave early tomorrow morning for Portus and then home. Everything that I've learned has only broadened the circle of people I've discovered in Ostia. Instead of narrowing the field at each point the circle gets bigger. I have one more avenue to pursue today with Philo's help. In all honesty, I don't think I'll be able to help your family. I can tell you this. I'm not sure how to tell Philo."

"Philo is my baby, my younger child, but he is now the pater familias. In one day he changed from a young man to an adult and the nominal leader of our family. Learning to handle unpleasant truth is part of that responsibility. He admires you. I see it in his eyes. You are the first man that has gained his true admiration. Oh, he loves Sabinus as his uncle. But, you. You light some spark I haven't seen before. I think he will listen to anything you say, even a disappointing reality."

"I'll tell him when I ask for his help. There's one more possibility."

Aemilia leaned even closer, paused, and then returned to her upright position. "Remember, disturb no more important families. Hints and aspersions to our friends don't help me. Philo is young. Sabinus is, well, Sabinus, a good man for business but no leader. Our position has shifted with Pius' death. I'll be frank. I liked my position as his wife. If you disturb the balance at this crucial time, I could lose my importance. I don't want to move to Rome and disappear in a sea of matrons. I like being queen in a small town."

Argolicus said, "I understand your feelings. I made a promise to Philo, and therefore to you. I'll do my best, in the time I have here, to discover who killed your husband. I'll take your suggestion and tread more lightly but I will still probe."

"As long as you understand."

"Which is more important to you, finding Pius' killer or your reputation?"

Aemilia shifted on the bench, her bracelets clinking against her wrist as she put her hand on the cushion. "Oh, now I see why you make people uncomfortable. You ask direct questions."

"I do."

"As long as Pius' killer goes unknown our family lives under a cloud of suspicion. People will wonder what caused someone to stab him. As I think about it, your finding the killer will restore our family name by bringing suspicion and doubt to resolution. Yes, find his killer but go softly."

"I shall do everything in my power for the rest of the day, to uncover the man or woman who killed him." Argolicus paused and smiled at Aemilia. "And, as you instruct, I will go softly. And now I'll find my tutor and then talk to Philo."

❦

Upstairs in his room, Argolicus found Nikolaos packing the few things they had brought to the villa.

"Master, I was straightening up for tomorrow. I left your things on the table." He nodded toward the table with the pen and the vellum.

"Let's look one more time at everything we have regarding this murder. Where are your notes?"

Nikolaos reached into a deep pocket and brought out his scraps.

"Lay them out on the table. We have just a few hours left."

Nikolaos set the vellum scraps in rows across the table arranging them in order from the beginning to this morning's meeting with the patricians.

Argolicus watched and said, "As of yesterday, we eliminated most of the family. Titiana is the only one left with hatred because of her friend Pacilus. But killing does not seem in her nature. She is rightly angry, and that is all. This morning we met some of the men we know were part of Pius' circle of corruption but not all of them. I just talked with Aemilia and she seems not to know how decadent Pius was. I'm not the one to tell her."

"Why not? You usually tell the truth no matter who it touches or how it touches them."

"On the other hand, I *do* have some sympathy. She's holding on to her position as the matron of Ostia. What good would it do to tell her? She knew he held parties for his friends. Why go into specific details? Otherwise, her sense of Pius is cool and evaluative. She, better than any of the rest of the family, knew how he manipulated people. Let her mourn and be free."

Nikolaos placed the last vellum scrap on the table, then stood back to look.

Argolicus continued, "Aemilia will survive the least wounded. Titiana will harbor her tainted vision of her father. Philo has been shocked into a reality he didn't know existed."

Nikolaos nodded and then pointed to the sheets spread on the table. "We found only some of the men..."

"Yes, and our questioning this morning started a train of reactions. There's the ruffian and the threat. That's straight-forward. We need to find who sent him. More unsettling is that rumors have started that I am disturbing the patricians here. Aemilia wanted me to stop searching at all. She felt her position here in Ostia threatened."

"To stop? Stop altogether?"

"Yes, until she realized that finding the killer would lift the shadow over the family name."

"Since the other men Pacilus mentioned are out of town, that leaves only the boys for us. Is that your next pursuit?"

"Something, something doesn't ring true. I can't imagine a boy of Philo's age or even that of Pacilus hiring a man to threaten me. It's possible. Money can buy anything. But it's the act of a mature man, not a boy. That ruffian looked like a man who could go well beyond a mere threat and has done so in the past. If we pushed harder, I'm certain it could happen and in a less public way."

"So, do we forget the boys?"

"No, not at all. I was ruminating. We'll get Philo to tell us where we can find them. Bring that scrap. What were their names?"

Nikolaos picked up the sheet. "Nobilier - naval officer. Macrinus - unknown. Arsenius - Promagistrate. Otho - silk merchant. Who knows, they may be out of town, too."

"The Promagistrate is back, so we know his son is here. If he's as burly as his father..." Argolicus realized he was speculating and stopped. "A naval officer, he must be connected with Portus. If they live in Ostia, we're in luck. We don't have time to cross the river again. Otho may be our best hope. His father must serve the matrons here with silks at a cheaper price than in Rome. Let's hope Philo knows Macrinus, and that he is here in Ostia."

"A strange place, this Ostia. It's the center of nothing," Nikolaos said. "The commerce here seems to survive by serving the patricians who still come here."

"I'll be relieved to get home to the country far away from any of the tentacles of Rome and its undercurrents." He sighed. "All this because of a favor to Boethius."

Nikolaos pocketed the vellum sheet. "Shall we find Philo, then?"

CHAPTER 10

EVERY MAN MUST MAKE HIS
OWN DECISION

Aemilia and Asina were talking in the entertainment room as Argolicus and his tutor passed through the *peristylum* on their way to the office. Sunlight fell in an afternoon slant from the open ceiling onto the plants and tiles of the big room. Servants passed carrying food and drink to the entertainment room. Sabinus and Philo were in the office, but they had ceased looking at accounts. Each of them sat in silence staring at the books on the table.

Argolicus told them about the morning in the forum, his conversations with the men, and his disappointment in finding no clues to Pius' murder except the encounter with the ruffian.

"But you are describing Asina's man, Altan. Everyone in Ostia knows him and stays clear of him." Philo said, astonished. "When you see him on the street, you know trouble is about to happen. He's not exactly a bodyguard, he's more of a problem solver. He collects debts when they are overdue. I know little about these matters but I hear he settles accounts for brothels when someone hasn't paid or is too rough with a girl. I'm not as naïve as everyone thinks." He turned his young face now marked by dark circles under his eyes toward Argolicus.

"Asina's man?" Argolicus replied. "Philo, think. Is there any reason this man Altan, would come to see your father? He is strong." He paused and paced in front of the table. "But he is a mercenary paid to do bidding. One quick stroke would be his way. He appears to know how to do violence, but efficiently. Whoever killed your father was angry... very angry. Those wounds suggest passion, not cold calculation."

Philo started to speak but Argolicus waved his hand to silence him. He continued pacing back and forth in front of the table. Then, stopped. "When did Asina return from the south?"

"Yesterday, from what I hear," Philo said.

"If that ruffian, Altan, is his man, why would he caution me? Does he work for other people? Patricians in Ostia?"

"Not that I know. But, now Asina will find someone for us. He is professional. The Promagistrate finds and arbitrates. His men are trained."

"Was he good friends with your father?"

"He came here for dinners. They did some business together. I just saw here," he pointed toward an account book, "that Father sold him some fabrics straight off the ship so Asina didn't have to go through a fabric merchant."

"That's exactly the way Pius did things," Sabinus said. "He would tell me to pull certain items from the warehouse. And, that is how he cultivated friends. He gave favors and expected them in return. It's how he grew and maintained his power."

Argolicus rubbed the sore spot on his chest, remembering the grab and the threatening warning. "Let's go see him. He's with your mother."

A tray of *gustum* snacks accompanied by honeyed wine now sat on a table in the entertainment room between Aemilia and Asina. Titiana sat by her mother's side.

"... and so you won't have to be involved. These men will work to find..." Asina was saying but stopped when Argolicus, Philo, and Sabinus, trailed by Nikolaos appeared in the archway. The Promagistrate twisted with a questioning look at the group.

"Ah, Asina. You haven't left. I had a question," Argolicus said.

"Yes?" Asina's face was blank of emotion.

Aemilia glanced at Argolicus to caution him not to push.

"I'm piecing together a chronology. When did your ship arrive?" Argolicus said, moving into the room. Aemilia frowned at him. The Promagistrate stood.

"My ship? My original ship was to arrive yesterday. But I tired of the provinces and returned three days early. Why do you ask?" Asina stood taller as Argolicus moved into the room.

"And did you see Pius when you returned?"

"Yes, yes, I did. I sent a messenger to set up a meeting, and he came to my house." Asina paused as his eyebrows squeezed together. "We met, we talked. He..."

"And your meeting was successful?"

"We came to an agreement. We..." Asina paused again, pressed his lips together, and shook his head back and forth. "No, we disagreed."

"You disagreed about your son, Arsenius? You were upset."

Asina stood still. His enlarged pupils darkened his deep brown eyes. He sat down, then stood up again. Aemilia and Titiana leaned forward as Philo and Sabinus moved closer to Argolicus.

"Arsenius?" Philo said startled. Titiana looked up with recognition as her eyes met Argolicus' glance. Asina sat.

"Yes, Arsenius," Argolicus answered. "Your son, Asina.

Your son told you something while you were away. He told you something that made you hurry back to Ostia."

"Arsenius," Asina said, shifting in his seat as his voice broke. "My son. Pius. My friend, Pius. Because of Pius my son lost…" His hands tightened into fists at his side. "My son, he seduced my son. Arsenius will never be the same. That is not friendship." He put his head between his hands. "I came in behind the slave with the fish. There was a boy. I asked him to find Pius."

"What are you saying?" Philo asked, his young eyes gleaming out of the dark circles. "You came here to harm my father? You, the same man who tried to seduce Pacilus, Titiana's friend? You hypocrite."

"I made a choice," Asina said, his body losing its authoritative bearing. Everything that had been tight slackened. "Arsenius had no choice. He was beguiled, forced. Pius, your father, told him if he did… if he… Pius told him it was nothing, the physical act. He told Arsenius that he would sponsor him. That of all the young men in Ostia…" Asina's eyes glistened with tears, his mouth turned down in sorrow. Then he took a breath, closed his eyes, and sat still.

Then he leaped up, eyes on fire, blinking back the tears. "Yes. Yes, I killed him. That liar and seducer. I was there to confront him. Pius came out of his room and we met in the *peristylum*." He gestured out toward the big room. "He made the same argument as you, Philo. But, my son, my son… had no choice. Every man must make his own decision. He said in time Arsenius would understand and that I would understand. I said it was rape. It *was* rape. Insidious mental rape first, then the physical act. That's the way Pius dealt with everyone. He twisted thoughts and made every bargain come out in his favor, even a young man's virginity."

"And the knife?" Argolicus asked. "Romans are forbidden

by law to carry weapons. Only the King's people carry weapons. You must have come with thoughts of murder."

"It was night, I was on the streets alone. Who would notice?" Asina said. He sat down again. "We're far from Ravenna. This is a Roman town. I don't know if I set out to kill him. I wanted to confront him. Killing him could have been in the back of my mind. I was angry. I wanted amends. But when he started with his excuses of power..."

Sabinus interrupted, "We will strip you of everything. We'll take this to court and win unequivocally. Our family will have justice." He pulled Philo next to him. "Look what you have done to this boy. He's distraught with grief, overwhelmed with discoveries about his father."

Aemilia sat stock still, her face composed in Roman dignity, and said, "Asina could be anyone Pius touched." She signaled to a slave, "Get N'Golo to show this man out." She folded her hands in her lap and watched Asina crumble into his silks in front of her.

Titiana rose and pulled the stunned Philo toward a bench. She wrapped him in sisterly arms as he stared out at the middle distance.

❧

ARGOLICUS AND NIKOLAOS READIED FOR THE SHIP TO Squillace in southern Italy long before the family was up for the funeral. But a haggard Philo discovered them in the vestibule as N'Golo was removing the large bar on the door to let them out. Philo opened his mouth to speak but instead rushed to Argolicus, embracing him.

Argolicus put his arms around the young man and then gently pushed him back.

"Find the facts. Think about them first, putting your emotions aside. Use them to your advantage."

Philo nodded.

"Know yourself and trust your sense of justice. You will be a man much different from your father and your own man."

Philo looked at him with trust in his eyes. "Thank you. Thank you. Without you... I've learned so much. You are welcome in our home always."

Argolicus picked up his bag and nodded to N'Golo. The big man pulled open the door. Nikolaos slipped out into the predawn gray. Argolicus said, *"First say to yourself what you would be; and then do what you have to do.* Epictetus said that. I'll send you a book."

AUTHOR NOTE
THANK YOU!

Thanks for reading *The Roman Heir*.

If you enjoyed *The Roman Heir*, please consider telling your friends or posting a short review. Word of mouth is an author's best friend and much appreciated. Thank you.

You wouldn't be here if you didn't like a good mystery and diving into another time.

I love to hear from readers. Send me a message at **zara@zaraaltair.com**

Want to know when the next story is out? Join the **Fans of Argolicus**. Get a free copy of the Argolicus mystery *The Peach Widow*. I'll personally let you know what's going on with new books and share some information about the world of Argolicus. http://bit.ly/ArgolicusReader

Now that you've discovered Argolicus, we bet you can't wait for another exciting puzzle. To satisfy your craving, turn the page and read the first chapter of THE VELLUM SCRIBE . . . .

THE VELLUM SCRIBE
An Argolicus Mystery
by Zara Altair

Arrival

Argolicus pulled back from the hit. How his older, smaller tutor Nikolaos was able to best him at swordsmanship mystified him. He grabbed his left side under the ribcage.

"Ah, Master, you must keep your defenses both up and down," Nikolaos said. "However much you cannot carry a weapon in public, knowing how to fight, and fight well, is mandatory."

Argolicus nodded. He'd been hearing this since he was a boy. And practicing since he was a boy, he was never as skilled as Nikolaos no matter how well they trained.

"You are right, Nikolaos," he put down his sword and walked toward the water barrel lifting out the ladle and sipping greedily. The exercise yard was between the main villa and the outbuildings of the estate where animals and slaves lived. To the south, Argolicus could see the sea sparkling in the early morning light. Below the estate, a road ran up from the port and town to the residences, like his, situated in the hills.

"Enough," he said, rescuing his pride. "Let's eat."

He heard a squeal and then laughter from his mother on the other side of the villa. He dropped his sword and ran. Nikolaos ran behind him still carrying his practice sword.

In the entry, his mother was lost in the hug of a huge man draped in brown robes. Behind him, a carter was unloading several wooden boxes, placing each one carefully on the ground.

"Uncle," Argolicus cried in Their Language. His face broke out in a spontaneous smile.

The big man turned. "Argolicus. The Father and the Son together!"

"Worship and glorify," Argolicus responded. "Uncle Wiliarit, where have you been this time?" He embraced his uncle who reciprocated in a hearty hug, squeezing him into the large chest.

Wiliarit continued in the language of The People, "I've been in Constantinople working on a commission. But now I'm here to finish and I'm hoping Nikolaos will help."

Nikolaos heard his name and came closer, still clutching the practice sword. Beside keeping Argolicus in practice with arms, he was an excellent grammarian and had taught Argolicus Greek since childhood. But, his language skills stopped at the tongue of King Theodoric and his people.

"Nikolaos?" Argolicus replied.

"Yes, he knows much about plants and herbs. I'm hoping he can point out some live specimens for illustrations. What I have now as a source are drawings in another manuscript. I want this one to be as excellent as possible. It is quite a large commission."

❧

Argolicus put down his pen and knife and looked up from his calligraphy of The People's language when he heard Nikolaos calling his name from outside the villa. Wiliarit, his uncle, had chastised him for not practicing writing and set him to calligraphy work with the Ostrogothic language. He glanced down at his work and frowned at his lack of skill. Wiliarit was right. Neglect was obvious.

But now, Nikolaos was closer and his calls were urgent. "Master! Master!" He arrived panting in the study.

"What is it? I thought you were looking for flowers." Argolicus said, standing up from his table.

"We are. We were. But down in the Angel's Meadow there's a body. Come quickly."

"A body? Do you mean someone is dead? A dead body?" Argolicus shook his head.

"Yes, yes. A young man, just like you. His face is blue. You must come and see."

Argolicus nodded, found his cloak against the cool late March air, and followed Nikolaos along a maze of animal trails over a hill to a verdant meadow. Here and there wild-flower colors - yellow, purple, blue, red - protruded among the green of early grasses.

Wiliarit stood in his dark brown robe in the middle of the meadow ignoring his unopened box of paints and vellum sheets beside him. His head was bowed and his arms uplifted in prayer.

The Used Virgin

The Peach Widow

The Vellum Scribe

ABOUT THE AUTHOR

Zara Altair is an emerging author of historical mystery. This is Zara's third book in the Argolicus Mystery Series.

Zara Altair combines mystery with a bit of adventure in the Argolicus mysteries. *The Roman Heir* is another story in the series of mysteries based in southern Italy at the time of the Ostrogoth rule of Italy under Theodoric the Great. Italians (Romans) and Goths live under one king while the Roman Empire is ruled from Constantinople. At times the cultures clash, but Argolicus uses his wit, sometimes with help from his tutor Nikolaos, to provide justice in a province far from the King's court.

Zara Altair lives in Beaverton, Oregon. She is a fiction author writing in the historical mystery genre. Her approach to writing is to present the puzzle and let Argolicus and Nikolaos find the solution encountering a bit of adventure and some humor in their search. Her stories are rich in historical detail based on years of research.

Stay in Touch
www.zaraaltair.com
zara@zaraaltair.com